Bilingual Edition
READING POWER
Edición Bilingüe

Óscar de la Hoya
Gold-Medal Boxer
Boxeador de medalla de oro

Rob Kirkpatrick

Traducción al español
Mauricio Velázquez de León

The Rosen Publishing Group's
PowerKids Press™ **& Buenas Letras**™
New York

To you, the reader.
Para ti, el Lector.

Published in 2002 by The Rosen Publishing Group, Inc.
29 East 21st Street, New York, NY 10010

First Bilingual Edition 2002
First Edition in English 2001

Book design: Maria Melendez

Photo Credits: pp. 5, 11 © Simon Bruty/Allsport; p. 7 © Ken Levine/Allsport; p. 9 © Holly Stein/Allsport; pp. 13, 15 © Al Bello/Allsport; pp. 17, 22 © Stephen Dunn/Allsport; p. 19 © David Cannon/Allsport; p.21 © Mike Powell/Allsport.

Text Consultant: Linda J. Kirkpatrick, Reading Specialist/Reading Recovery Teacher

Kirkpatrick, Rob.
    Óscar de la Hoya : gold-medal boxer = Óscar de la Hoya : boxeador de medalla de oro / by Rob Kirkpatrick : traducción al español Mauricio Velázquez de León.
    p. cm. — (Reading Power)
    Includes index.
    Summary: Introduces the Mexican American boxer whose skills won him a gold medal in the Olympics.
    ISBN 0-8239-6149-4
    1. De la Hoya, Óscar, 1973– Juvenile literature. 2. Boxers (Sports)—United States Biography Juvenile literature. [1. De la Hoya, Óscar, 1973– 2. Boxers (Sports) 3. Mexican Americans Biography. 4. Spanish language materials—Bilingual.] I. Title. II. Series.
    GV1132.D37 K57 1999
    796.83'092—dc21
    [B]

Word Count:
English: 125
Spanish: 124

Manufactured in the United States of America

Contents

Contenido

Óscar de la Hoya is a boxer.

———

Óscar de la Hoya es boxeador.

Óscar grew up in Mexico. He lives in the United States now. Óscar likes Mexico and the United States.

_____

Óscar creció en México, y ahora vive en los Estados Unidos. A Óscar le gustan mucho los dos países.

Boxers throw punches.
Óscar can punch with his
left hand, and he can
punch with his right hand.

————————

Los boxeadores dan
puñetazos. Óscar puede
golpear con la mano
izquierda, y puede
hacerlo con
la mano derecha.

Boxers wear robes when they go in the ring. They wear gloves when they box.

———

Los boxeadores visten una bata cuando suben al cuadrilátero (ring). Además usan guantes para boxear.

Óscar likes to go to the gym.

———

A Óscar le gusta ir al gimnasio.

13

Sometimes boxers sit down to rest. They sit down in the corner of the ring.

———

Algunas veces los boxeadores se sientan a descansar en una esquina del cuadrilátero.

Boxers get belts for big wins. Óscar loves to win belts.

———————————

Los boxeadores ganan cinturones por sus triunfos. A Óscar le encanta ganar cinturones.

Óscar boxed for the United States in the Olympics. He won a lot of fights.

Óscar representó a los Estados Unidos durante los Juegos Olímpicos. Óscar ganó muchas peleas.

19

Óscar won a gold medal in the Olympics.

Óscar ganó una medalla de oro en los Juegos Olímpicos.

21

Óscar just loves to box. He is a good boxer.

A Óscar le encanta boxear. Es un buen boxeador.

This is a good book to read about Óscar de la Hoya:

Para leer más acerca de Óscar de la Hoya, te recomendamos este libro:

Oscar de la Hoya: A Real-Life Reader Biography
by Valerie Menard & Valene Menard
Mitchell Lane Publishers (1998)

Web Sites

Due to the changing nature of Internet links, PowerKids Press has developed an online list of Web sites related to the subject of this book. This site is updated regularly. Please use this link to access the list:

Sitios web

Debido a las constantes modificaciones en los sitios de Internet, PowerKids Press ha desarollado una guía on-line de sitios relacionados al tema de este libro. Nuestro sitio web se actualiza constantemente. Por favor utiliza la siguiente dirección para consultar la lista:

http://www.buenasletraslinks.com/sports/delahoya

Glossary

belts (BELTS) What boxers get when they win fights.

corner (KOR-ner) The place in the ring where boxers go to rest after each round.

gloves (GLUVZ) What boxers wear on their hands.

gold medal (GOLD MEH-dul) What you win when you are the best at a sport in the Olympics.

Index

Glosario

cinturones (los) Premios que obtienen los boxeadores cuando ganan peleas de campeonato.

esquina (la) El lugar en el ring donde se sientan a descansar los boxeadores después de cada asalto.

guantes (los) Lo que usan los boxeadores en las manos para pelear.

medalla de oro Premio que ganas cuando eres el mejor en un deporte en los Juegos Olímpicos.

puñetazos (los) Los golpes que dan los boxeadores con los puños.

Índice